NOT SCARED OF THE DARK

CONNOR WHITELEY

No part of this book may be reproduced in any form or by any electronic or mechanical means. Including information storage, and retrieval systems, without written permission from the author except for the use of brief quotations in a book review.

This book is NOT legal, professional, medical, financial or any type of official advice.

Any questions about the book, rights licensing, or to contact the author, please email connorwhiteley@connorwhiteley.net

Copyright © 2023 CONNOR WHITELEY

All rights reserved.

DEDICATION

Thank you to all my readers without you I couldn't do what I love.

CHAPTER 1

Absolutely nobody knew what Ares Marsius would be when he was older and after he had been fighting for the glorious Emperor for tens of thousands of years, but everyone had forgotten his name now. Nobody remembered what heroic acts he did before, nobody remembered how much he loved the Emperor. Nobody was even allowed to mention him outside of how evil he was in the military.

Now everyone only remembered how many trillions of innocent people he murdered each year as the leader of the Traitor Superhumans against the Emperor, and how he only wished to enslave humanity for their own slow agonising death.

But it wasn't always like that.

About fifty years before Ares turned his massive superhuman back against the Emperor, he stood on his massive black oval bridge filled with tiers upon tiers of baseline humans hunched over their holographic computers typing, swiping and talking away as they did whatever was required of them.

Ares had always loved how massive his black blade-like flagship was, the bridge alone was so immense it took even a superhuman Angel of Death and Hope over two minutes to run from one side to another, it was that big, but Ares's absolute favourite feature of the bridge had to be the giant floor-to-ceiling windows that allowed him to stare out into the cold darkness of space.

The sound of people talking, their light footsteps tapping the rough marble floor as they made their way about the immense bridge and the sound of someone shouting orders all made Ares smile, because his amazing crew was at work, hard work for him, the Empire and the amazing Emperor he loved beyond all else.

As much as the constant foul aroma of walnuts, cloves and rich bitter coffee irritated Ares' superhuman senses, he supposed that as long as the human workers keep working hard, it was just something he was going to have to put up with.

Sadly.

Ares might have been over three metres tall, fully cladded in pure blue thick Angel armour that was styled on the armour of medieval knights and always carried two massive almost-oversized black battle-axes on his back, but he loved how much he preferred the humble nature of non-superhumans for they were warm, loving and caring.

Something he was always trying to improve

himself. He always made sure that his people were protected, safe and secure, and to the surprise of the other 8 Angel legions he never ever engaged in the enemy unless he had a concrete plan or just knew that he was going to win.

He fully admitted that he was strange like that but being the unofficial favourite of the Emperor, Ares just knew that it was the strategy the amazing Emperor would have chosen to.

That was why Ares was staring out over the vastness of space. On the orders of the Emperor's Council Ares had summoned his entire legion, drawing them from all four corners of the Empire, to the galactic north to the Nihilus System, a very large solar system home to over two hundred worlds and trillions of humans on each planet.

He wouldn't have entirely minded that the damn summons (sometimes he just felt like some dumb puppy whenever the Council *summoned* him) but Ares was really hoping to partake in his favourite little hobby, creating amazing robots and metal creatures that looked identical to real flesh and blood humans. It was of course as illegal as hell, but it was so much fun and he was surprisingly good at it.

And if he worked a little too much on that pet project than Ares had really, really wanted to study up on some languages, both alien and human dialects, some of his superhuman friends might have called him a nerd, but he loved knowledge.

For knowledge was power.

Ares really liked watching all ten thousand of his blade-like warships gather into position with him above the capital world of the system, an immense green planet covered in thick jungle and lustrous blue oceans.

The Emperor's Council had apparently believed there was a full-scale rebellion being raised in the system against the divine Emperor so they had wanted Ares to investigate. Just the mention of some idiots wanting to rebel against the Emperor just pissed him more than life itself.

Ares just couldn't see any pathetic reason for rebelling against the Emperor. The Emperor was kind, generous and worked every single bloody day to make sure all of his subjects were in the best position they could possibly be at.

"My Lord," a woman said from behind Ares.

Ares nodded and the young woman (she was only two hundreds years old to Ares' 70,000 years old), Ares was so glad that Commander Georgia of the Empire Army had decided to join him on his mission.

Ares had first met Georgia on an Emperor-forsaken jungle world in the far south of the Milky Way, they had fought together for ten straight years against an aggressive alien foe together, and she had proven herself worth more than a hundred baseline men, she was a furious fighter that was a certainty.

And if Ares and his superhumans were going to be fighting another enemy on a jungle world that Ares just wanted, needed her by his side. And it was also pretty great that Georgia was the head Commander of a full detachment of Empire Army soldiers, so that was at least another twenty thousand soldiers to help Ares against the foul traitors to the Emperor.

"My Lord Marsius," Georgia said, "the Council was wise to put you in charge and how many forces do we have to play with?"

Ares looked at her for the first time since she had come aboard, and it was always so interesting to see the dark blue uniform of the Empire Army, offering no protection, security or usefulness in comparison to Ares's own superhuman armour.

But that was the thing about the Empire Army, as much as Ares hated it, sometimes they were merely human-flesh-shields to keep the enemy busy whilst Ares and his superhumans did the actual crippling work.

"Full legion strength," Ares said, "so a million superhumans and your twenty thousand soldiers,"

Georgia gasped and Ares could understand why. It sort of made sense for baseline humans to be so concerned about numbers but Ares just had a feeling that if the Emperor's Council of all things wanted him at all Legion strength then something major was going on.

Ares turned and focused on all his command crew hunched over their holographic computers.

"Get me the Supreme Commander of the System's Defence Force," Ares said.

Everyone stopped and Georgia folded her arms.

"My Lord," Georgia said. "That is why I came to see you first, there is no military left in the entire system. All soldiers, security guards, weapons on all two hundred worlds are dead,"

Ares's eyebrows rose. He had been in plenty of theatres of war over the thousands of years of his life, but this was the very first time that he had ever been to a warzone where all the military was dead.

"I reading reports saying there was an entire detachment of Angels here," Ares said.

Georgia frowned. "My Lord, that's the point, all ten thousand Angels stationed here from the Galaxy Burners are dead,"

If Ares was a normal human then he fully expected himself to let his mouth drop, sweat pour off him or to do another pathetic human action. But he was a superhuman first and foremost, he couldn't show any emotion, but the Galaxy Burners were some of the fiercest superhumans in the Empire, no one just killed them all.

But someone or something had slaughtered over ten thousand superhumans with such ease that Ares had no idea what could have done it.

And that scared him more than he ever wanted to admit.

CHAPTER 2

Commander Georgia just couldn't believe how absolutely amazing luck that the Lord of War himself, Lord Commander Ares Marsius of the Angels of Death and Hope had actually summoned her of all people to his aid. That was just so amazing that she couldn't believe how excited she was.

Georgia stood in Ares' wonderfully large oval bridge with the tiers upon tiers of hunched over workers that worked so tirelessly in service of the God Emperor on their holographic computers. It was so great to be here breathing in the wonderfully scented air of walnuts, cloves and rich bitter coffee that came from the mugs of the human workers, that all left the most sensational taste of coffee cake on her tongue, just like how Georgia's mother made when she was a tiny girl. Those really were amazing days.

The others talking, tapping and shouting of orders was a little surprising and not what Georgia had expected from the flagship, The Demigod, from one of the best fighters in the Empire. Georgia had been expecting something calmer, more controlled, but considering she was probably only one of a handful of Empire Army officials allowed on the bridge, she wasn't going to complain.

And she had heard of Ares killing people who insulted him anyway.

Even the Lord Of War himself looked like a divine demigod that would burn an entire sector of space with a simple look of his icy cold blue eyes, but even she had to admit the two massive battle-axes scared her a little. Georgia always felt the need to bow in the presence of such a god but Ares had told her off in no uncertain terms when she first did that after two years of fighting together, she didn't dare make that mistake for the next eight years.

But it was just such an honour to be fighting alongside this god of a superhuman for this amazing battle.

And this was far, far better than her original idea about returning to the newest Empire Army recruitment world to play blackjack, go clubbing and even read up on the latest findings on what the foul enemies of the Emperor were planning.

But Georgia definitely preferred blackjack first and foremost.

And as much as Georgia wanted to believe that even the God Lord of War could claim victory here, she wasn't sure as she reread the reports and showed them to Ares about the ten thousand dead Angels.

Georgia had reread the reports over and over because the entire thing was just so impossible to imagine. No one killed that many superhumans it was impossible, absolutely impossible, but she had seen the photographs herself.

Somehow something or someone had killed so many Angels that it was an official record for the most superhumans to die.

A record that had to be avenged.

"Contact the Planetary Governor for the Capital World," Ares said to her.

Georgia swiped her dataslate a few times and swiped towards the rough marble floor in the centre of the oval bridge. A few moments later a very tall elderly man appeared in holographic format just frowning in utter shock at Ares.

"My Lord Of War, it is an honour," the man said as he knelt before his god.

Georgia completely understood the feeling.

"What is the information you provided the Emperor's Council? What is the status of the system?" Ares asked.

The Governor shrugged. "That is unknown my Lord of War. We send the reports of the dead Angels and dead military then we lost contact with all other worlds in the system. We cannot contact each other. Our ships cannot take off. We cannot do much of anything,"

Georgia just folded her arms at the Governor.

How the hell could this happen to such an amazing system? The Nihilus system was a masterful hub of warship production, Empire Army recruitment and it produced so much for the Empire it couldn't afford to fall, and it was so well protected Georgia just couldn't understand what the hell was happening.

"Where did this start?" Georgia asked firmly.

She had quickly learnt before that when standing next to a superhuman it was best to act as tough as she possibly could.

Ares nodded for the governor to answer the question.

"I do not know Madam, the entire system went down together. And we can only contact you now because your equipment seemed to reverse the effects of the… we don't know what it is, and remember you contacted us first,"

Georgia slowly nodded. Clearly whoever the enemy was, they were clever and had great knowledge about the communication and computer systems of the Empire. If a human was behind this then they had to have something from Mars or another Martian-owned world on their team.

If an alien race was behind this, then Georgia didn't want to consider how smart and deadly they were.

"Where did the reports of rebellion start?" Ares asked.

The Governor shrugged. "Unknown,"

Georgia just looked at Ares. This governor was

one of the most useless and futile ones she had ever met, and Ares didn't look like he disagreed.

"Would knowing where the first group of Angels died help you?" the Governor asked.

Ares took a few booming steps forward. "Tell me,"

The Governor looked as if he was about to wet himself.

"Nihilus 57 my Lord of War," the Governor said. "And according to my engineers this world lost communication a tenth of a second before every other planet did,"

"Thank you," Georgia said, "The Emperor Protects,"

"The Emperor Protects," the Governor said before Georgia cut the link.

Georgia folded her arms and just looked at Ares.

"He was as useful as a wet paper bag," Georgia said, not sure if Ares would understand the ancient reference she had learnt from historical documents.

"I agree but the enemy was clever. Knocking out communications, stopping ships from working and killing off the defenders of a system. Exactly what you would need to do to invade a system," Ares said.

Georgia almost smiled at the twinkle of light and impressiveness and respect that Ares had in his eyes. He was clearly impressed with the enemy, and so was she.

But she just had absolutely no idea who they were facing. It was impossible to imagine some mere humans could knock out a system's communications, let alone the rest of the terror acts, alone.

So who were they facing?

Georgia just looked at Ares and he nodded.

"All forces," Georgia said. "Head to Nihilus 57 immediately,"

As the bridge became a hive of activity once more Georgia just stared out of the massive floor-to-ceiling windows and into the darkness of the cold void.

Whatever answers they needed Georgia and demigod Ares had to find them. Georgia just knew the fate of the Empire rested on them bringing these monsters to justice.

CHAPTER 3

As Ares stepped out of the immense jet black blade-like shuttle with twenty other extremely well trained Angels of Death and Hope firmly behind him, Ares stepped out onto the icy cold red soil of Nihilus 57.

The entire planet was shrouded in pure darkness that Ares could see because of the advance nigh-vision capabilities of his Angel armour.

Ares stood in the middle of an immense bare landscape that seemed to stretch on endlessly without a hill, animal or anything to even suggest that they were somewhere that wasn't entirely flat. The air was made of up a strange composition of nitrogen and oxygen that would make even the smallest of sparks explode into a raging fire within seconds. Ares didn't want to fire a single shot from his superhuman gun unless he absolutely had to.

He had already noticed a few of the new members of the Angels that had joined him on the journey to the planet's surface had questioned why he wasn't using his massive battle-axes, but Ares made a point never to use them unless he was actually in battle, and not just being wary in case of an enemy ambush.

But he wasn't entirely sure how safe or alone he felt in the vast expanse of the landscape. It wouldn't be easy for an enemy to ambush them but there was no cover, no protection, no nothing to help them if they were attacked. Ares really didn't like that.

He was almost glad that he had ordered Commander Georgia to stay on the Demigod and direct the fleet whilst he was away. She had been so shocked by the sheer privilege, that was such a typical human response, but Ares trusted her.

Unlike the other Angel legions that had their specialisations, like the Raven Crow legion were infiltration specialists and the Hydra legions were superhuman spies and other legions had their own abilities. Ares's legion did not, he much preferred to be masters of everything and not narrow in their focus to warfare.

Even through the advance filter system of the armour, Ares hated the smell of arid almost-nutty air that tried to burn the moisture away from his throat but his Angel biology stopped that from happening, if there were dead Angels on the planet than he had to find them, investigate them and collect their bodies for the Galaxy Burners to give their fallen Last Rites.

"My Lord scans show an energy field is

shrouding the planet, no light can penetrate the atmosphere," a short female Angel said.

Ares nodded he was glad that Captain Maya of his second company had been free to join him. She was a furious enemy on the battlefield and a master of arms and extremely loyal to him. She was like a gift sent from the Emperor to him.

"Advance," Ares said, "but be aware of the enemy,"

Everyone nodded and Ares led them forward. Their superhuman feet pounding into the dry red soil as they marched forward in search of the bodies.

"Pilot," Ares said through their communication system. "Take off and cloak yourself in high orbit, we do not want you to be destroyed by the enemy,"

"Of course my Lord of War. By your will it shall be done," the Pilot said.

Behind them Ares heard the roar of the blade-like shuttle's engines power up then the shuttle started to fly away.

It exploded.

Ares spun around. Massive chunks of flaming wreckage rained down hammering the red soil.

Ares raised his gun and scanned the area. Everyone else was doing the same.

The massive chunks of wreckage became immense fireballs as the extra oxygen in the atmosphere encouraged the fire.

Ares hated it that he couldn't detect anything. The shuttle couldn't have just exploded on its own, there had to be a reason for its death, Ares just couldn't see the enemy yet.

"We push onwards," Ares said, continuing to walk on.

He was never going to let some pathetic enemy forces scare him of all people into retreating. Ares was an Angel of Death and Hope, he was a superhuman crafted by the Emperor himself, he did not know fear, anxiety or anything for he was a demigod amongst little humans.

Ares adapted his walking as his feet pounded into much rough red soil that looked like it had been greatly disturbed lately.

Ares's helmet scanned the patterns in the sand and there was nothing regular about them. It didn't look like drag marks nor nothing else that Ares had encountered before.

Something deadly strange was going on on this shrouded world.

"My Lord," Maya said. "I cannot reach the Demigod or Commander Georgia. No communications can leave the planet,"

Ares was so glad he didn't bring any baseline humans on this mission. They probably would have moaned, panicked or screamed that they were completely alone on a strange world with a deadly enemy most probably nearby.

Ares wasn't scared in the slightest and neither were any of his Angels.

A few moments later Ares's night vision detected

a large group of corpses piled up on one another and his superhuman stomachs twisted in a knot at the very idea that some enemy was capable of destroying them.

It only took a few more superhuman strides to arrive at the pile, but Ares was definitely shocked at the way how the corpses in their blood red armour had been so carefully stacked on top of one another, for this wasn't a pile per se, it was a temple made from corpses.

Every single corpse of the Galaxy Burners had been constructed like bricks in a grand cone-like structure that rose high into the black sky like it was a hand reaching out to the heavens.

"No humans could have done this," Maya said.

Ares nodded. Each Angel weighted about 200 kilograms of solid muscle, armour and superhuman organs, it was impossible that a mere human could move over 500 of the Angels regardless of how many there were.

If this was in fact the very first group of Angels to be slaughtered then Ares hated to even imagine what the other groups of murders looked like.

Ares scanned the cone of corpses and noticed how none of the corpses had any signs of bullets, stab wounds or anything that would explain their deaths.

Ares had come here hoping to solve the mystery of the murders but he only had more questions. Like if someone was coming to murder superhuman Angels then why the hell stay around long enough to put their corpses in the shape of a cone.

The enemy had to know that the Angels did not know true fear and they couldn't be scared (even though Ares liked to use the term as a joke) so what was the point?

"Energy signatures are coming from inside the cone," Maya said.

Ares focused on the cone-like tower of corpses and his fingers tightened round the trigger of his gun as he noticed that the corpses were moving.

The corpses were glowing bright white as well but the light was coming not from the corpses but behind them.

The cone structure wasn't solid, it was hallow, so all that Ares could wonder was what in the Emperor's name was inside the tower of corpses?

CHAPTER 4

The very, very last thing Georgia had ever imagined possible was she of all people would be in charge of the legendary Demigod, Flagship of the Lord of War, merely stepping on board the ship was an immense honour that she would probably get a promotion over, but to actually command it, and seriously command all forces that Lord Ares had control over was something else entirely.

She was basically a god at this moment.

Georgia stood firmly in the very centre on the rough marble floor of the oval bridge as she listened to the tapping, swiping and mutterings of the tiers of workers doing whatever they were doing on their holographic computers. Georgia had ordered them to find out everything they could about Nihilus 57, what had happened and the status of their Lord and Master the Lord of War. But Georgia just knew that things were bad.

She had never had any idea about what to call her

sense for danger, but it had saved her life too many times for her to ignore it.

Georgia was already more than willing to send down every single ship they had down to the planet below in case Ares was in danger, but she was waiting. Georgia had learnt long ago when it came to new forces under her command she couldn't be seen to be overreactive.

She had to wait a little longer until she had more information.

But Georgia just had to admit how amazing she felt standing in the middle of the oval bridge in such a legendary warship. The most sensational thing about the Demigod was that it actually wasn't a Flagship by design, it was only an Annihilator class warship, so it could technically destroy entire planets, but this one was special.

Georgia loved telling others the story about how Ares had been trapped by an alien armada who had barricaded him within a solar system with it being impossible for reinforcements to enter. Ares had lost so many men and women to the aliens, and all his ships were lost.

Except the Demigod.

Ares managed to teleport onto the Demigod, help the last remaining forces kill the aliens on the ship and somehow Ares had managed to use his single ship to wipe out the aliens from existence.

And it was the moment Georgia had first heard the story that she had fallen in love with this mere god amongst men.

"Madam," someone said behind her.

Georgia stood up perfectly straight and looked up at the immense three-metre-tall black armoured Angel with a bright copper helmet.

Georgia didn't even bow to Ares's Shipmaster Charlie, a legend within his own right.

"Report Shipmaster," Georgia said coldly.

Charlie held up his dataslate and read it. "We have lost contact with the Lord of War the moment they entered the atmosphere,"

Georgia just nodded. It wasn't surprising in the slightest, but it just meant that her fears were coming true. This was hardly good.

"What about the planet itself?" Georgia asked, knowing that the scientists in the fleet had sent down drones to investigate the planet.

"Unknown Madam," Charlie said. "The Drones exploded the moment they touched some kind of energy field around the planet,"

Georgia folded her arms and went over to the massive floor-to-ceiling windows.

"Did the drones go down before or after Ares?" Georgia asked.

Charlie gasped, he was probably just surprised that Georgia had dared to use his first name.

"Before,"

Georgia smiled. That was good if the drones had gone down before then there was a chance that there was an energy field trapping Ares inside the planet.

Georgia was just glad that wasn't happening.

"My Lord!" a woman shouted from the top computer tier.

Georgia looked up.

"The shuttle's gone. I had a weak signal then it… exploded or something," the woman said.

Georgia slowly nodded making sure she looked perfectly in control of the situation. The very, very last thing she was ever going to do in front of superhumans and Ares's command crew was be emotional and weak and human-like.

"Scan the planet," Georgia said to Charlie.

Charlie hesitated.

"Shipmaster, I am in full command of the fleet. Do as I command," Georgia said.

Charlie nodded and swiped at his dataslate. Georgia looked away from the floor-to-ceiling windows and focused on the rough marble centre of the bridge that was humming as the holographic projectors roared to life.

"Displaying the results now," one of the command crew said.

Georgia forced herself not to even smile as a red hologram of Nihilus 57 appeared to show the planet completely shrouded in darkness.

Yet the edge of the atmosphere shone slightly.

"Madam," Charlie said, "there is some kind of energy being projected from a single spot on the planet but it is strong enough to make it impossible to scan the entire planet. There are no weak spots either,"

That was surprising, Georgia had absolutely never known a planet-wide energy field or shielding not to have any weak points.

Georgia paced around the bridge for a moment pretending to look thoughtful. But inside her heart was racing and her mind was travelling much faster than these planets were spinning.

She just had to save the Lord of War. Something was deadly wrong here and absolutely nothing made sense of this mystery so far.

But her sense for danger was growing stronger and stronger each passing second. Ares was in trouble and his entire team was in mortal danger, she had to do something.

"We need to conduct an extraction," Georgia said.

Even though Charlie was wearing a helmet, Georgia just knew he wasn't sure on her and his eyebrows were raised.

"No one extracts the Lord of War Madam," Charlie said.

"And tell me Shipmaster has Ares ever allowed a mere mortal to control his forces before?"

Charlie folded his arms. "Negative Madam,"

Georgia just stared at him. "Then trust me. Lord Ares is in mortal danger and if we do not save him the entire Empire will be in danger,"

Georgia had absolutely no clue if the last bit was true but she just needed the added dramatics.

Charlie stayed silent for a long moment before nodding. "I can have two military transports available within a minute,"

"Make it five Shipmaster," Georgia said.

"Of course Madam," Charlie said as he walked away.

Georgia turned her back at him and simply stared down at the shrouded planet below and just wondered what the hell was going on.

And most importantly if the only hope for humanity was still alive. If he was how much longer could Ares survive.

Georgia just hoped the transports would hurry.

CHAPTER 5

Ares was amazed and so badly wanted to face and kill and slaughter whatever foul creation or beings were inside the evil cone-like tower of corpses.

The air was crisp now, cooler and Ares just wanted to fight in the Glorious Emperor's name, and he was definitely going to get revenge on these creatures for daring to kill 500 of the Galaxy Burners here. Killing an Angel of the Emperor was the very worse sin to Ares and he was not going to let these creatures on unpunished.

The bright white light continued to shine out of the awful cone-like tower of corpses and Ares carefully placed his superhuman gun on his waist and took out his two black massive battle-axes. He wasn't kidding around here and all the twenty other Angels around him simply tightened their fingers around the trigger.

Then the light stopped.

Ares went to step forward but that was probably

what the enemy wanted, yet it was equally strange that the shuttle was destroyed, there was an energy field blocking off communications and the entire planet was shrouded in darkness.

It wasn't even like Nihilus 57 was too far away from the system's star, it was fairly close actually, and this planet used to have thirty Earth-Standard hours of sunlight. A long time to be honest.

Ares raised his battle-axes and pointed them at the tower of corpses.

All nineteen Angels around him readied, aimed and fired.

As superhuman bullets screamed through the air, Ares just watched and waited for the results.

The bullets exploded into the tower of corpses and whilst it felt like a complete disrespect to his follow Angels from another Legion, Ares could see that their Legion Lord would appreciate the destruction. A sort of symbolic way for the Galaxy Burners to go out in style.

As the chunks of their Angel armour and flesh and brains charred and smouldered, Ares just used his helmet's night vision to zoom in on the bodies.

There was nothing inside the tower of corpses.

"My Lord," Captain Maya said coming up next to him. "Scans show nothing inside the bodies and our equipment didn't even register the light we all saw,"

Ares just looked at her, that had to be completely impossible.

"Keep trying to signal the Demigod. There is

nothing useful on the world. This world is dead, the corpses are useless and this mystery just gets bigger and bigger," Ares said.

He really wanted to lash out and killed something to channel his rage at them. It was bad enough he was having to face these corpses that could have been anyone under his command, but the mysteriousness of the killing just annoyed him further.

Ares went over to the corpses and just stared at the dull lifeless faces. He actually remembered fighting side by side with some of them thousands of years ago, but no more. For they were dead. And he couldn't even help them find closure.

"Movements close by," Maya said.

Ares raised his battle-axes. He felt something here too, something in the wind, something in the air, something watching him.

Something, not someone.

Ares ducked. A blade rushed past him.

Ares spun around only to see that nothing was there. There was no person, no alien or even any sign that the air had moved around him.

But Ares had felt the air move or something to show that a blade had rushed past.

He saw his Angels do the same but as he watched them he could see there were absolutely no enemies attacking them.

Something was certainly playing tricks on their superhuman minds, but Ares had always expected this kind of rubbish from baseline humans, not Angels of

Death and Hope.

But Ares would figure it out. He just knew he could.

Again he felt the air change. It twirled around him. He felt a sword swinging towards him.

Ares waited.

It was so close. Ares waited.

Ares spun around.

Smashing into something.

A shadow screamed. More blades rushed at him.

Ares couldn't see anything. He was fighting on instinct.

Ares swung his axes. Smashing into enemies.

Tens of blades came at him. Ares swirled. Ares swung his axes. He killed something.

Ares kept fighting.

More blades attacked.

Angels fought. Angels screamed. Angels died.

A blade slashed Ares's back. Ramming into his shoulder blade.

Ares didn't stop. He spun around. Swinging his axes.

He killed something.

Everything was a blur. He still couldn't see the enemy.

Bright lights exploded overhead. Five bird-like shuttles zoomed towards Ares.

Ares saw the enemy in the light. Massive beasts made from shadow.

They dived forward.

Tackling Ares to the ground. They smashed their claws into him. Ares's armour screamed.

Ares whacked them away.

The shuttles landed.

One exploded.

Ares jumped up. Smashing his axes into the enemy.

Ares heard people shouting at him. He had to get to the transport.

A beast grabbed him. Throwing him to the ground. Stomping on his head.

Ares's helmet shattered. Ares ripped it off.

Swinging his axes at the beast. Slaughtering it.

Ares ran towards a shuttle.

Two more exploded.

Ares kept running.

It started to takeoff.

A beast chomped on his leg.

Ares swung his axes. Shattering its skull.

The shuttle was higher now. Its engines were failing.

Ares ran faster.

He jumped into the air.

Grabbing the shuttle.

The shuttle zoomed away.

CHAPTER 6

Georgia was just stunned as she stood in front of the large glass window outside the Medical Bay on the Demigod, she hated seeing the rows upon rows of black armoured Angels having the medical Angels that were dressed in sterile white armour having to operate on them, carefully removing their armour and just trying to make sure their superhuman biology survived.

The entire medical bay took up an entire immense level of the Demigod, and this was the first time ever that Georgia had heard of this many Angels being treated, but all nineteen Angels that had tried to protect the glorious Ares had been infected with something, and now the medical Angels were trying to stop it.

Even as Georgia stood in the perfectly cool little room outside the medical bay, she could still smell the aromas of decay, rot and ultimately death. It was impossible for everyone in the Empire to become sick from bacteria, viruses or fungi from other planets because the extreme vaccination requirements the Empire had in place to make this impossible.

Angels had even stronger immune systems so it was clear as day that whatever this was, it wasn't naturally occurring.

Georgia forced herself not to react as she realised that they were facing a biological weapon strong enough to kill even Angels of Death and Hope. Something that until recent days had just been absolutely impossible to imagine.

The sound of thumping, humming and screaming filled the air as various medical equipment and saws activated to force the Angels out of their armour. This was hardly good and Georgia just knew she had to return to the bridge as soon as possible but she had to make sure Ares was okay.

A sliding door to Georgia's right hissed and she smiled as the massive three-metre-tall Lord of War walked towards her, and simply stood next to her.

Georgia still felt like she was in the presence of a god amongst men, but this wasn't the time for worship or admiration. This was a time to find out what the hell had gone wrong.

"Are you cleared my Lord?" Georgia asked.

Ares was still wearing his immense black helmet over his face but Georgia had a good feeling that he was smiling at her, impressed at her commitment to professionalism given the situation.

"Of course Commander," Ares said with a

mocking tone.

Then Ares gestured Georgia to follow him, and the white metal wall behind her revealing a secret cylinder lift that Georgia would guess led to the bridge.

Georgia went in first then Ares followed.

"What happened my Lord?" Georgia asked.

Ares shrugged as he closed the lift's doors.

"I read the reports, saw the footage and had to contact Earth Command on the situation, but what is your report to a friend?" Georgia asked.

Ares raised his hands to his helmet and a hissing filled the lift as the pressured air escaped from the helmet, he took it off, revealing a very scarred but immensely impressive face that was almost beautiful, if not stunning in a superhuman kind of way.

Ares smiled at Georgia. "I do not know what we face. The enemy thrives in the darkness, the shadows and is faster than anything I have ever seen before,"

Georgia couldn't say anything. That was certainly the impression she had gotten from the footage from the shuttles and the reports from the survivors before they were rushed into the medical bay.

"Why didn't you get infected?" Georgia asked.

Ares smiled. "The Emperor in his divine wisdom was extra careful with us Legion Lords. He gave us abilities that mere Angels would never have. My immune system is extreme even for Angels, but I can confirm this is a biological weapon and I now have a feeling how the Galaxy Burners died and the military too,"

Georgia grinned. That was flat out amazing news and now they were dealing with a biological weapon then that was a serious advantage over the enemy.

Georgia faced Ares and leant against the icy coldness of the metal lift.

"A biological weapon isn't easy to make and security getting into the Nihilus system is tighter than more solar systems," Georgia said.

Ares folded his arms.

"So it had to be made in system meaning the aliens or traitors are still here and they were created in the system," Georgia said.

Ares didn't look sure about her assessment of the situation, but Georgia knew she was right. About a hundred years ago she had tried to bring in a ton of biological weaponry into the solar system so she could gift it to Mars for research (and new equipment), and the amount of red tape she had to go through was ridiculous. The Nihilus system was probably no different.

Georgia felt the lift start to slow down and she was just glad she would be in the bridge soon so she could test her theory.

"If that is true," Ares said, "then there are still two hundred planets to investigate. We have the resources so it will take time,"

Georgia's communicator on her wrist buzzed and she answered it.

"Madam," Charlie said. "Three planets around

Nihilus 57 have gone dark. We cannot communicate with the worlds, all Empire forces are presumably dead and… another ten planets are just gone dark,"

Georgia just looked at Ares. It was surely impossible for so many worlds to go dark at once, there were 14 planets now lost to the Empire. That was just crazy and strange and unpredictable.

"We have to make progress now," Ares said.

Georgia completely agreed but how in the world where they meant to? They had no information, no clues about the alien they were facing (Georgia was sure it was an alien at this point) and she wasn't sure how the hell they were meant to fight it.

The lift came to a stop and Georgia felt her stomach tighten into an agonising knot.

They were running out of time and millions of people were probably dying because of it.

And Georgia still had no clue whatsoever who or what they were facing.

CHAPTER 7

Ares was absolutely furious at these alien bastards for daring to attack so many worlds dedicated to the glorious Emperor. This was just outrageous that they were stupid enough to be this pathetic, weak and arrogant at the righteousness of humanity.

Humanity was the only divine species that had the right to invade, conquer and slaughter in the vastness of space. It was humanity and Angels of Death and Hope that were the masters of space, not some pathetic alien abomination.

This ended now.

Ares went into the massive oval bridge and stomped over the rough marble flooring in the middle of the bridge, and just went straight over to the immense floor-to-ceiling windows. Ares wanted to so badly take out his two black battle-axes and just thrusted them into something, channelling his rage, but he just had to focus for now.

Ares hated the constant aroma of strong bitter coffee that his damn command crew loved so much, but for now at least he needed them.

Ares turned to face the tiers upon tiers of hunched over command crew working at their holographic computers, and he clicked his fingers.

Moments later an immense red hologram showing the entire Nihilus system with the worlds that had gone dark in bright, almost blinding, purple.

Georgia came over to him, Ares just loved it that she was here. She was probably one of the few people she could trust to handle this situation with him, and she had been clever enough to know something was wrong, and Georgia had saved him.

"What is so special about these worlds?" Ares asked.

"My Lord," Charlie said standing on the other side of Ares. "These worlds are all former Fortress worlds, dedicated to the focus of protecting the inner layers of the system,"

Ares didn't care. He had fought on so many Fortress Worlds over the millennium that after he had fought on the first twenty, they had become too dull because they all looked the same.

And there was absolutely nothing to protect besides some forge worlds and the capital world of the system. But a biological weapon was probably perfect to use on former Fortress worlds, yet it was strange how when Ares had gone onto the planet, there was no sign of any structures, which was impossible for a fortress world.

"Why did you say Former?" Georgia asked.

"Madam, only because they're destroyed," Charlie said.

Ares rolled his eyes. He was really hoping that Georgia had just asked the critical question that would unlock everything.

"What about the history of this system?" Ares asked.

Ares flicked his wrist a couple of times and the hologram twisted, swirled and twirled in front of him as the system changed going back millions of years to when alien life was first detected or thought to have been present in the system.

Ares managed to go back to about a million years before the very first humans had developed on earth, and he was surprised to see back then the Nihilus System only had a hundred planets.

"My Lord," Charlie said, "according to the Ordo Historicus, they found evidence of an alien empire in the system that lasted for about two million years before they disappeared,"

Ares folded his arms. That could be critical in this mystery, and if thousands of years had taught him anything it was that no race or enemy just disappeared.

"Describe these aliens to me," Ares said.

Ares was about to listen to Charlie answer him when he heard the bridge's door open, and Maya staggered in wearing bright red crimson armour that was definitely stained with her own blood.

As much as Ares wanted to tell her to go back to the medical bay because she clearly wasn't used to the cybernetic replacement for her left leg (at least he hoped that was what caused the staggering), Ares just needed every single intelligent person he could find.

Maya was definitely intelligent as his second in command.

"The aliens in question," Maya said, "were called the Nilihusian, bestial creatures that were ruled by a theocracy and their belief in a great Lord of War that would rise from the ashes of a dead empire and would claim the galaxy as their own, rewarding the Nilihusians for their dedication to their Divine Lord of War,"

Ares instinctively took out his two massive battle-axes and Georgia whipped out her pistol on his waist.

Everyone gasped but the Angels on the bridge aimed their weapons at Maya.

Ares just knew this wasn't Maya in the slightest. She never staggered, she never referred to him by his title, even if she was recalling some kind of historical text, Maya was not human anymore.

"Relax divine Lord of War," Maya said, "your children are spreading throughout the Medical Bay. We will rise up to help you conquer your species and then we shall rule the galaxy because you are the Divine Lord of War rising from the ashes!"

Ares charged forward.

Maya didn't move. She reacted. She smiled.

Ares jumped into the air. Swung his battle-axes and slaughtered Maya where she stood.

"Lock down the medical bay," Georgia said a moment before Ares could.

"My Lord!" Charlie shouted.

"Fifty warships from Nihilus Defence Force has appeared calling for the Divine Lord of War," Charlie said.

Damn it. Ares hated this, he wasn't a god or anything but these aliens were spreading thick and fast, infecting everyone he knew and loved.

"Another hundred warships," Charlie said.

Ares quickly calculated the numbers. A hundred and fifty warships were all that remained in the Nihilus System after the initial destruction of military and Angel forces.

But that begged another question. The military were all dead so who the hell were controlling the warships?

CHAPTER 8

The rich aroma of sweat, burnt oil and Maya's dead body filled the entire oval bridge as the command crew hunched even more over their holographic computers and set to work on trying to discover in the Emperor's fine name what was actually going on.

Georgia flat out couldn't understand who on earth was powering, controlling and trying to contact them using the Nihilus Defence ships that were smaller blade-like warships compared to Angels's warships, but they were still powerful.

Georgia stood firmly next to Ares as they both monitored the entire fleet of their own forces as they moved into a defensive formation to protect the Demigod in case the foul outrageous enemy decided to seal their fate and fire. The Demigod and Georgia's own forces would easily survive, but the enemy or whatever they were would surely die a fiery death.

Georgia had already wanted to open fire and kill

them all but Ares was absolutely right about wanting to find out some information first.

What they needed was a way to learn more about what the hell was actually going on.

"My Lord," Charlie said, "the fleet has completed formation. I have raised our shields 20%, our weapons have locked onto the warships and our Annihilators systems are fully charged,"

"Are they haloing us?" Ares asked.

Georgia was rather impressed Ares did not look at Charlie once, he simply continued focusing on the fleet through the immense floor-to-ceiling windows, whilst Georgia subtly noticed Ares's hands were twitching, almost like he wanted nothing more than to simply whip out his battle-axes and use them on the enemy.

Georgia knew the feeling all too well, this was so much better than playing blackjack and clubbing.

"Yes my Lord,"

Georgia went over to Charlie who was standing in just off the centre of the oval bridge.

"Put them through," Georgia said.

Everyone in the bridge stopped in utter shock that she would dare give an order instead of allowing Ares to speak.

"Do as she commands," Ares said, still not looking away from the fleet.

Georgia just glared at Charlie until he obeyed.

"Putting them through now," Charlie said.

The massive holographic projectors in the bridge

hummed to life and even the Demigod protested a little as a massive ape-like creature appeared in red holographic form.

"You not our Lord," the Ape said to Georgia.

Georgia didn't bother speaking to the alien. She was impressed it could speak the Empire tongue rather well, but there was a cruelness to how he twisted it on our unhuman tongue.

But maybe that was why the aliens, the Nilihusians, had chosen an ape-like form, at least that way their voice box would be somewhat similar to those of humans.

"But I am," Ares said as he came over to stand next to Georgia.

Georgia felt like her knees would collapse at any moment, Ares was projecting such an aura of authority that all she wanted to do was kneel.

"You," the Ape said. "You not a shadow. You not gifted your birth right,"

Georgia just shook her head. Whatever this creature was, was clearly delusional and needed to be put down, yet she trusted Ares so he had to have a plan for this.

She just hoped she wouldn't have to endure this Ape much longer.

"How did you get onboard the warships?" Georgia asked.

The Ape laughed. "On-Board? Soft creatures gave us them. They worshipped our Gods, our Goddesses, our Prophets like you. They caused the darkness. They caused the peace. They caused us to awaken from the Eternal Sleep,"

Georgia's eyes widened. This was such a revelation, if she was hearing this correctly, the Nihilus system had willingly handed themselves over to Nilihusians, including their warships and everything else. But why did the Planetary Governor of the Capital World tell Earth about the deaths and rebellion?

Georgia just looked at Ares as it looked like he had worked it out too, but his expression was more subtle in a superhuman kind of way. The Planetary Governor of the Capital World had wanted Lord Ares here for the sole purpose of probably making him realise his destiny.

"My Lord," Georgia said, "we are deep within the Nihilus system, now enemy territory, and the entire system has fallen into Rebel hands,"

The Ape might have been shrouded even in holographic form but Georgia just knew that it was smiling and watching her, trying to size her up to see if she was a threat or not.

She was definitely a threat, of that she vowed she wouldn't allow these aliens to live.

"Activate the fleet," Ares said. "Destroy them all,"

Georgia just smiled as the entire command crew and bridge became a hive of activity, all whilst Georgia and Ares stared at the abomination of the shrouded Ape.

"It is your destiny!" the Ape-like creature shouted.

Ares took out his battle-axes. "I decide my own destiny,"

The Ape creature laughed but there were other creatures laughing with it. Tens if not hundreds of creatures laughed loudly.

Georgia tried to cut the link but it wasn't working.

The Demigod screamed as its systems were strained and the hologram flashed repeatedly.

Then massive shadowy Ape creatures walked through the hologram and just stood in front of Georgia and Ares.

The enemy was here.

CHAPTER 9

Ares was absolutely furious with these evil, foul and horrific abominations that dared to defile his Great Human Empire and the glorious Emperor. Ares was not some prophet or god or anything that would dare take what rightfully belonged to the Emperor, all these massive ape-like creatures shrouded in shadowy darkness were pathetic fools that just needed to die.

Ares whipped out his two massive battle-axes and watched as the small tide of ape-like creatures poured onto his large oval bridge.

Ares rushed forward.

Angels triggered their guns. Firing.

Ares zoomed towards the apes.

The apes charged.

Ares attacked. Swinging his axes. Chomping into their flesh.

Apes died.

Others attacked. Ares ducked. Ares swung. His

axes hacked at the enemy's flesh.

Heads shattered.

Bodies exploded.

Blood painted the marble floor.

Ares kept charging.

More apes came from the hologram. He couldn't see Georgia.

He hoped she was dealing with the hologram.

An ape tackled Ares.

Ares spun around. Whacking off the ape's head.

Ares charged more.

More apes attacked. Charlie raced past Ares.

The apes pounced on Charlie. He screamed.

A superhuman arm was ripped off.

Ares raced over.

Apes jumped in his way.

Ares slaughtered them.

An ape tackled him to the ground.

Ares snapped the ape's spine over his knee.

Ares raced over to Charlie. Slaughtering the apes attacking him. Charlie was injured. But alive.

Command crew members screamed. They were being massacred.

Ares saw apes climbing up the tiers. Ripping his command crew apart.

Ares didn't hesitate. He only acted. Ares charged over to the tiers.

He climbed on them. Beheading any enemies he came across.

Blood poured down from the tiers. Creating a

lake on the floor. Ares didn't care.

Ares kept climbing. Kept killing. Kept saving the command crew.

A massive hand grabbed Ares's leg.

Throwing him across the bridge.

Ares smashed into the floor-to-ceiling windows.

Ares saw an immense ape the height of the bridge charge at him.

The ape roared.

Ares rolled away. The ape grabbed him.

Trying to crush him in his armour. Ares couldn't move. Couldn't fight. Couldn't anything.

The lights went off.

The air became thin.

The hologram turned off.

Ares fell to the ground.

A few seconds later when the lights, the envirosystems and the holographic computers reactivated, Ares just smiled in cold contempt as he saw that the hologram serving as the portal for the Ape-like creatures was dead.

And the Apes were no longer attacking through the hologram.

Ares carefully placed his battle-axes on his back armour and thankfully a system's diagnostic on his Angel armour revealed he was perfectly okay, and his armour was already starting to heal itself.

"My Lord," Charlie said weakly from the centre of the oval bridge.

Ares rushed over to him. It was unthinkable for a

Legion Lord to feel so much love for a member of his legion but Ares just cared about everyone who served under him. He couldn't let Charlie die, not that Ares knew for certain he was dying.

Charlie just laid there on the cold rough marble floor as Ares knelt down next to him, his dark black armour covered in thick red blood, some of it human from the command crew, some of it a very almost black red blood from the shrouded ape-like creatures, barely clinging to life.

Ares held him in his arms as he noticed that Charlie's superhuman biology was already starting to heal his wounds, like the loss of his arm and the massive teeth marks in his chest and stomach.

Whatever these Nilihusians were they were monsters, that was as clear as day, not that the Nihilus system was actually getting much sunlight these days.

Ares listened to the constant muttering of Charlie as his superhuman side tried to heal himself, but that primal human part of all Angels that no matter the implements or the psycho-conditioning could ever truly remove was trying to deal with the trauma of what had just happened.

Because what had just happened defied all human logic.

Ares had studied, fought and killed slightly over a thousand different alien species in his extremely long life, and he had never encountered an alien race that could materialise through holograms, turn entire worlds dark and corrupt humans into open worship.

But that was now the true problem, Ares, his entire legion and all of Georgia's forces were deep in enemy territory with a planetary governor that had sold the system out to aliens.

"Ares," Georgia said as she limped over to him after entering from the door to the bridge.

Ares heard a bunch of Angels and surviving command crew members mutter about her cowardice and her running away from the battle but that all stopped when they noticed the rather deadly burns on her hands.

Ares just saluted her as he realised that she had ran out of the bridge to access the panel where thousands of volts of pure electrical energy coursed into the oval bridge.

Georgia must have pulled out the cables, stopped the hologram and reconnected the cables a few seconds later. Meaning she had thousands of volts coursing through her for a few seconds.

An act most deadly and something that could have killed everyone else on his ship, besides Ares. Maybe Georgia was stronger than she looked.

"Did I do it?" Georgia asked.

Ares just nodded and focused on the immense sea of blood and human corpses around him.

It was only then that Ares realised that over half of his command crew was dead, his shipmaster was heavily injured and the medical bay was still in lockdown because of the infection that had made Ares kill Maya.

Ares liked the warm touch of Georgia's soft hand on his armoured shoulder (the benefits of having a touch-sensitive suit of armour) and he almost wanted to lead into it.

But Ares was the Lord of War, second to the Emperor and the salvation of humanity. Ares had to figure out what their next move was.

All before the enemy striked again.

And now that the enemy realised Ares wasn't their prophesied Lord of War rising from the ashes they would kill him.

Of that Ares had no doubt whatsoever.

But Ares just looked forward to killing them ten times harder. And he certainly didn't need some dumb prophecy to tell him that.

CHAPTER 10

Georgia was extremely looking forward to the absolutely wonderful medical bay reopening just so she could get her hands attended to. They hurt like hell and the skin on her hands were crispy, blacken and Georgia wanted to scream in agony, but she was amongst Angels so she forced herself not to.

The air stunk of grapefruits, lemons and limes as Georgia sat in a small oval room with just herself and the almighty Lord of War in his black armour and this time his two impressive battle axes were placed against the warm white walls of the room.

Georgia really wished she shared his confidence that no one would dare to interfere with their little meeting and mini-lunch (or whatever the real time was), but Georgia seriously didn't.

Instead Georgia put her black booted feet up on the freshly polished brown oak dining table that was shaped in another oval and just smiled at Ares as he looked at her. He was probably wondering if she was being "bad" or whatever according to normal humans.

Georgia wouldn't have actually minded playing some blackjack or even poker on the oval table. It was perfect for the game and Georgia felt like relaxing, but the mission was far too important for that.

"The capital world has to be important," Georgia said.

Ares looked up from his little plate of red, blue and yellow fresh fruit and nodded.

"I agree," Ares said, wiping his mouth. "Do you want a plate?"

Georgia nodded and Ares flicked his wrist and a large plate of freshly sliced strawberries, lemons and grapefruit materialised in front of her. Georgia was really impressed, this sort of replicated food was almost impossible to get in the Empire Army for an influential commander like herself, let alone the half-starved troops.

"I think we should order the fleet to go to the capital world," Georgia said. "But what happened to the Nihilus Defence force's warships that appeared earlier? I was too busy focusing on the apes and by the time I returned from the power adventure they were gone,"

Ares cocked his head for a moment and then looked to the ground and finally looked at her.

"You're right," Ares said. "After the apes in the bridge, I was focused on cleaning up, finding replacements for the command crew… and of course your forces engaged the enemy and they retreated,"

Georgia smiled. As the commander in charge here she really should have checked in with her forces, but the entire situation was so mad she had forgotten.

A mistake she couldn't make again.

"When we make it to the capital world," Georgia said, "the enemy will attack us but *you* must make it onto the planet's surface,"

Ares took another mouthful of his sliced fruit and shrugged. "Why me?"

Georgia took her feet off the table and leant forward with such bad posture her former Commander would have whipped her.

"Because my Lord, you need to kill the Planetary Governor and find the truth," Georgia said.

"And you my dear," Ares said, "will need to command the orbital offensive,"

Georgia picked up a cold damp piece of sliced grapefruit gingerly to stop the pain of her hands from increasing. "I can do that my Lord. The enemy will burn in my fire and the alien shall know the Emperor's wrath,"

Ares flicked his wrist again and two glasses of bright green liquid appeared in front of each of them. They smelt amazing but Georgia was a little curious what the drinks were.

"To our health," Ares said, downing each glass in one.

Georgia picked up the icy cold glasses (subtly biting her tongue as her hands felt like they were killing her) and just wondered about all the reading, scanning and studying of defences she was going to have to do in the next few hours.

It would take about three hours to reach the capital world of the system and the enemy would predict that was their next target.

There would be no element of surprise so whatever happened Georgia had to be ready and had to be fully in control.

Georgia just looked at Ares who was studying her, probably looking for any signs of weakness or doubt or failure. But as she downed her two extremely tasty, if not deadly healthy, drinks she absolutely knew he didn't find any because Georgia would not fail Ares, for he was a god amongst men, impossible to kill and a leader she would happily die for.

Georgia just hoped today wouldn't be that happy day.

But she couldn't be sure.

CHAPTER 11

The smell of fearful sweat, burnt ozone and blood filled the massive oval bridge as Ares stood in the very centre of it on the rough marble floor gripping his battle-axes as the entire legion and Empire Army forces prepared to breakout of Slidespace, their primitive warp drive technology.

Ares hated this entire planet and system but he just knew that he had to get down to the planet below, find the Planetary Governor and find out what the hell was going on.

According to more and more foul scans of the systems over eighty percent of the worlds in the system had gone dark, and the tidal wave of darkness was quickly approaching the capital world, and Ares "feared" that if they didn't act now then they would lose the only person who could answer his questions forever, because if the Nilihusians had taught Ares anything over the past day or two, it was that they would happily kill anything that got in their way.

Ares had absolutely no intention of being another tally to their kill list.

"Activating Teleporters!" Charlie said as he limped over to the immense floor-to-ceiling windows standing next to Georgia.

Ares just smiled as he waited for the rush and excitement of exiting Slidespace and then him and the twenty other Angels he had handpicked throughout the entire ship would be teleported down.

Ares seriously hoped the teleporters would work perfectly this time and not scatter them throughout the capital world, but that was definitely not a given.

"Bring us another two degrees," Georgia said. "Raise shields to max. Charge weapons now. Dial back engines and rediverted the power to the weapons. Let's slaughter these bastards,"

Ares was so glad he had her on his side. If he was a normal human then he might have almost felt sorry for the enemy, but they deserved everything they were going to get.

"Cut Slidespace engines… now!" Georgia shouted.

The bright green and blue capital world appeared in front of them. Thousands of enemy ships were suddenly working and orbiting the world.

They were zooming towards Ares's forces. Unleashing their fighters. Ares just couldn't understand how all the Planetary Governor's ships were suddenly working in the system.

"Teleportation target locked," Georgia said.

"Launching!"

Ares loved it as the entire Demigod hummed, popped and vibrated as blue smoke swirled around him.

"The Emperor Protects!" Georgia said.

Ares saluted her as he teleported away.

NOT SCARED OF THE DARK

CHAPTER 12

Georgia was so glad the amazing medical bay was open now, so she finally managed to get her hands repaired.

The entire cold void of space exploded into a bright array of fiery deadly colours as Georgia ordered their forces to slaughter the enemy. Georgia hated seeing so many blade-like shuttles, fighters and warships turned against the righteousness of the Emperor and his loyal servants.

Georgia just wanted, needed them all to be masterfully slaughtered so she could finally turn this ugly, annihilated system that had fallen from so much divine grace into a hulk of its former self, over to those that were actually loyal to the Emperor could restore this immensely impressive solar system back to the Emperor's righteous vision.

"Incoming!" Charlie shouted.

Georgia snapped back to reality. She stared out over the immense expanse of the void and focused on twenty annihilator missiles bombing towards them.

"Defensive Formation 2," Georgia said.

The entire fleet hummed to life as every single fighter was launched and all the cruisers, warships and more spun to their correct position.

Georgia loved how now every ship was arranged into a perfect prism.

"Fire," Georgia shouted.

The Demigod roared to life. Cannons smashing into the enemy. Ripping out chunks of their hulls.

Slaughtering the missiles.

The enemy returned fire. Georgia gripped anything she could.

Some of the command crew fell over. She waved them to get back up. She needed them.

A bright blue hologram appeared in front of Georgia.

She studied it. The hologram highlighted enemy movements.

Georgia swiped away at it. ordering ships to fire on different targets.

Red flashing lights exploded on the bridge. They were losing ships.

Georgia checked her Empire Army forces. 25% of them were annihilated. Their forces floating in space.

Georgia needed a new plan.

A massive explosion lit up space. Georgia looked at it. An immense petroleum transport exploded.

That shouldn't have been there. People were

trying to escape the planet.

Enemy ships exploded as the petroleum burned their hulls.

More transports were leaving the capital world.

Georgia had to make a choice. Use the escaping petroleum transports to kill the enemy. Or allow the people using them to escape.

Georgia didn't know if they were friendly or not. They were probably the enemy going off to spread the Nilihusian's corruption to other systems.

They had to die.

Georgia ordered the entire fleet to fire on the transports.

The entire orbital battle around the capital world became a fiery inferno. Enemy ships crackled like logs on a fire.

Ships ripped themselves apart as their engines exploded.

Alarms exploded on around Georgia. Something was coming.

Georgia saw a massive missile heading towards them. One that could easily wipe out the bridge.

Georgia spun around. Charlie was relaying orders. She had to do something.

Georgia turned back to the hologram. Ordering a cruiser to evacuate. But it didn't.

The cruiser zoomed in front of the Demigod. Becoming atomised as soon as the missile struck it.

The cruiser had sacrificed itself for her.

Charlie ran over to her. Pointing to something on

the hologram.

There was something coming up from the capital world. An immense group of blade-like five warships.

Georgia had never seen anything this large. These five ships were gigantic with weapons to match.

The five ships fired.

The Demigod rocked violently. Ships around it shattered like glass.

The enemy ships were recharging.

Georgia just looked at Charlie. This wasn't good. She had to destroy those five ships before it killed them.

There was no other choice.

CHAPTER 13

Ares almost choked on the overwhelming, almost suffocating stench of rotting flesh, lavender and pine as he rematerialised in a long white marble corridor with golden trim lining the walls to add even more regalness to the palace.

Ares focused on the absolutely awful orbs of bright white light that hovered high above him near the top of the ceiling, but he was at least somewhat interested that he came to three metres tall and the ceiling was at least three times taller than him. Ares just didn't know if that was a waste of space or some clever design trick.

The only damn problem with the teleportation was that it was becoming deadly clear that the twenty others he had picked to join him were scattered through the palace, or worse the entire planet.

"My Lord," a familiar voice said over the communication network. It was a captain of a company that Ares had picked.

"Confirmed," Ares said as he took out his two black battle-axes and started stalking the corridor.

"Me and the others are in the hanger of the palace. Approximately two kilometres from your position," the company captain said.

Ares just rolled his eyes. That was hardly the sort of news he had been wanting to hear.

"Make your way to me as soon as possible," Ares said cutting the link.

Ares heard two male voices coming up ahead where the corridor seemed to bend to the right and moments later two white robed men came out holding a pile of dataslates each.

"We must make sure the enemy who not reach the surface," one of the men said clearly not knowing Ares was there.

Ares threw his battle-axes.

They smashed into the chest of the two men and stuck them to the marble walls behind them.

Ares went over to the heavily bleeding corpses that were certainly dead and Ares just ripped his battle-axes out, allowing the corpses to fall to the ground like they were nothing. Because that is exactly what they were.

Ares knelt down for a moment and picked up a couple of the dataslates the two men had been holding. He ordered his armour's computer systems to hack them for information and then he streamed the information in front of his eyes.

He was just grateful for the superhuman ability to

absorb information at extremely fast rates compared to other humans.

Ares hated that the dataslates were useless.

"What's that?" a female asked.

"Dunno," another said.

Ares spun around. He saw three heavily armed women run at him.

They fired.

Bullets pounded his armour

Ares charged.

He swung his axes. Ripping into their flesh. Slaughtering them.

A rocket slammed into Ares.

Throwing him back.

Seven more women charged at him.

Ares jumped up. The rocket dented his armour. Damn them.

Ares flew forward. Swinging his axes. Ripping into flesh.

Women fought. Women screamed. Women died.

Some women leapt over Ares. Slashing his back armour. It was useless.

Ares punched them. Shattering their skulls.

Brain matter exploded out.

Ares kept killing until they were all dead.

After a few moments Ares just stood there for a second or two admiring all the hacked-up corpses, blood that painted the walls as an almighty testament to his power and he just knew he had to press on for the Emperor.

Ares continued stalking the corridor as it stopped curving round and went perfectly straight leading towards a very large golden door.

The closer Ares got to the golden door the tenser he felt, it was almost like the door itself was trying to tell him that it was dangerous, unsafe and he should flee for his life.

But that wasn't Ares. Ares was a Lord of War and he never cowered from a fight with the enemies of the Emperor.

Ares went straight over to the golden door, running his armoured fingers over the loving warmth of its smooth surface and it simply fell open.

Then it dissolved.

Ares raised his axes as he entered the bright orange room that was easily the size of a football pitch, and Ares really didn't like it.

He hated the bright ugly orange of the roughly textured walls with odd dark art on the walls that didn't contrast the orange in a positive way. Ares absolutely hated the strange sculptures depicting slaughtered humans on the spires to strange gods or being from space.

Ares just wanted to burn this entire palace to the ground but he had to find the planetary governor and…

Ares looked over to the other side of the bright orange room and saw a very yellow dining table that was almost large enough to land a shuttle on, and right in the middle was the freshly roasted corpse of the planet governor perfectly seasoned with thyme, rosemary and garlic.

Ares just shook his head as he focused on the three alien beings shrouded in shadows as they carefully sliced off pieces of the Governor's cheeks, placed them on their plates and seasoned them with a splash of lemon.

"Sit down Lord Ares," one of the aliens said. "We have much to discuss,"

Ares had absolutely no clue what he had just walked in on but he definitely knew this was the place to get answers about everything.

He just wasn't sure if the answers were going to be what he wanted.

CHAPTER 14

This is one of the worst things Georgia had ever had to do before. There was absolutely no way in hell that she would or could survive this but she just had to try.

Georgia absolutely hated these alien bastards as they zoomed towards the Demigod in their five extremely massive blade-like warships that had already shattered the ships surrounding the Demigod.

Georgia had ordered more ships to replace them but they were busy dealing with the other enemy ships attacking them.

"Enemy canons almost charged," Charlie said.

Georgia seriously hated these newer "super destroyers" that were intent on slaughtering Georgia and her friends. But she had to survive and make sure the enemy was distracted from the Lord of War for long enough.

Georgia focused on the hologram in front of her. Tons of data streamed past her eyes. Their shields were already at the max and the enemy would shatter them.

That was the problem with Flagships. They weren't designed to be destroyers, cruisers or anything more than a very fierce command centre.

Georgia just smiled as she realised that the Demigod had been retrofitted to become a flagship for Ares.

But it had always been a destroyer and more specifically an Annihilator class destroyer. So few people knew that little detail.

One of the super destroyers fired.

The weapon blasted past them.

The Demigod rocked violently as the ships around it were atomised.

Georgia knew that Annihilator Class warships had extremely tough hulls. Making them perfect for smashing into other ships.

Yet the Demigod was old. She couldn't be sure if it would survive the impact.

She had to try. Georgia sent the calculations to Charlie standing next to her.

He didn't look sure but he nodded.

The super destroyers were about to fire on them.

Georgia pressed the orders into the hologram. Charlie executed the order.

The Demigod shot forward.

Enemy ships became blurs. The command crew screamed in terror.

Georgia saw something get closer.

Georgia realised they were about to smash into something. She didn't want to become a paste against the windows.

Charlie gripped her waist.

The Demigod smashed into a super destroyer.

The entire ship screamed in agony.

The windows cracked.

The super destroyer exploded in a sensational fireball.

The Demigod's shields were lost.

Immense chunks of wreckage flew towards the other super destroyers.

They exploded.

Humans flowed into the void. Aliens followed. All froze to death. Shattering as their corpses smashed into chunks of wreckage.

"Commander!" someone shouted.

The last surviving super destroyer zoomed towards them.

It couldn't fire.

The Demigod wouldn't survive another impact. Not without its shields.

Georgia didn't know what to do. She had to act. The command crew were clueless.

Charlie shrugged. It was up to her to save them all. She wouldn't lose this legendary warship.

She had to get the shields back up. She had to divert power once more but it could kill her.

Georgia just knew that. She couldn't survive absorbing all that power once more.

Georgia just had to try.

She raced across the oval bridge. The metal door opened for her.

Georgia flew out into a large endless pentagonal corridor running down the spine of the ship.

She went towards a small loose panel into the bright white walls. Taking it off. She saw the thick blue cable had fallen off.

That's why the shields had failed.

Georgia wanted to touch it. Plug it back in but she couldn't. It would cook her alive.

It was her life or the life of millions on these ships.

Georgia reached towards the blue cable.

A superhuman grabbed her. Throwing her against the wall.

Georgia saw a blur of black grab the cable. Georgia rushed over to stop the enemy.

The superhuman threw her again.

A deafening scream echoed down the corridor as Georgia realised Charlie was plugging the cable back into the socket.

The overwhelming choking smell of cooked flesh filled the air and after a few moments Charlie fell onto the bright white ground.

His helmet fell off revealing a charred, scarred face of a hero. Georgia just knew he was dying that there was no helping him this time.

Georgia wanted to touch his face, hold his massive hands and just do something so Charlie knew he wasn't alone when he died.

But Charlie just smiled through cracked charred lips at her and slowly nodded. He was saying that it was okay to leave him to die and that he had served his Emperor and sacrificed himself for him.

There was no greater honour.

Georgia slowly nodded and forced herself up. She never expected to feel sad, awful and regretful as Charlie, a challenging superhuman that only followed her orders because it was what the Lord of War commanded, died.

Georgia went back into the oval bridge and everyone looked at her in silence as the last of the super destroyers smashed into the Demigod's shields and shattered itself.

There was still a battle to win for Ares and the Emperor and everyone was waiting with bated breath for her next command.

For she was in full command and she fully intended to kill every single enemy that dared threatened herself, her forces and Ares.

"Kill them all," Georgia said coldly.

CHAPTER 15

This actually wasn't the strangest of things Ares had actually seen in all his thousands of years but there was still absolutely no chance in hell he was really going to sit down with these three shadowy aliens on their massive table with the freshly roasted planetary governor getting sliced up there.

"You can sit down," one of the aliens said.

It was just annoying that Ares couldn't tell them apart and all the aliens looked the same in their shrouded forms, as they sliced up the planetary governor, carefully placed the juicy slices on their plates and ate him.

The horrible smell of rosemary, thyme and garlic was just plain overwhelming and Ares was glad his helmet was managing to keep most of the smell away. But Ares's most unfavourite piece of the entire room had to be the foul orange roughly textured walls, they were simply abominations.

"Why aren't you attacking me?" Ares asked.

The aliens looked at him and laughed. It was a strange twisted laugh but Ares could still recognise it.

"Why would we attack you?" one of them asked. "We infect everything in the end, well except you, your biology is beyond weird for us,"

Ares just nodded. At least that explained what was going on with Maya, the outbreak in the medical bay and some of the other weirdness.

"What are you three?" Ares asked, subtly looking about for possible escape routes. He couldn't allow these three to escape.

"We are the Triumvirate of Nihilus," one of them said. "We are the original three that founded our Empire, infected the system and bent them to our will. All before making our infected offspring go off to their Great Sleep,"

Ares's grip on his battle-axes tightened. These people had to be extremely dangerous.

"We were rather happy to be honest sleeping until one of your *mining* companies, forgive me if I haven't pronounced it correctly, dug us on and attacked us," another one said.

Ares was starting to understand the subtle differences between the voices but not enough to pinpoint who was the speaker each time.

"You attacked an entire solar system for nothing," Ares said.

The aliens laughed as they started to slice up the planetary governor's well-toned stomach.

"Needs a little more seasoning," one of them said

as they sprinkled more garlic on the governor's stomach.

This was just disturbing.

"We had no idea that your species would take over much of the galaxy," someone said. "We had predicted something like your species would evolve but never that you would become space-going creatures. We visited earth and some other worlds before the Great Sleep but your worlds were pointless,"

Ares didn't know if that was a compliment or not.

Ares went over to the edge of the dining table and pointed his axes at the two closest aliens.

"Do you control all of them?" Ares asked referring to the people attacking his forces in orbit. "And how are you controlling them?"

The aliens just shook their heads and stood up. The air crackled with dark black power.

"We control everything using our hive mind. You are weak in fighting us. The ships and communications networks in the system were never down," they all said as one. "That was a clever lie designed by our roasted puppet here,"

Ares gestured he would attack as the aliens walked towards him.

The air crackled more and more then the shadows shrouding the aliens melt away revealing horrifically beautiful forms.

Ares had never seen such beautiful humans in all

his life. The two aliens closest to him were absolutely stunning women with bright blond hair made from starlight that shone like angel wings in the growing darkness of the room. And Ares seriously loved their bright white dresses that floated higher and higher revealing more of their sexy skin below them.

And the last alien wasn't a bad looking man but he didn't do anything for Ares. But he was still stunning and Ares almost felt like he would question himself, maybe men were gorgeous after all.

The darkness around Ares grew and grew and Ares looked outside through grand windows to see the entire planet was getting dark.

It was descending into pure darkness.

"It's beautiful," Ares said.

The two stunning women kissed Ares's helmet and he loved their erotic touching of his armoured body.

This wasn't real.

Ares forced his superhuman mind to focus and forget about the damn primal urges of humans. These were alien abominations.

Ares spun around.

Punching the two women.

Shattering one of their skulls.

"He's awake!" the man shouted.

"The Lord of War raises from the ashes of a dead system," the woman said.

It all made perfect sense now. The Nilihusians must have learnt about his title and abilities when the mining company awoken them and they attacked and they must have investigated the company's computer system to learn more about the new galaxy.

The Nilihusians must have found mentions of Ares and wanted to enact their prophecy, so clearly this entire thing was about killing off the Nihilus system and reducing it to ash so Ares could rise once more.

But the only way to destroy a solar system was to destroy the sun and get it to explode. It would slaughter the entire system and the Empire would never be able to use the planets again.

The man disappeared.

The woman launched herself at Ares.

Ares swung his axes.

Energy blasted out from her hand.

Throwing him backwards.

Ares smashed into the orange walls.

Ares rushed forward.

The woman was agile.

She leapt over him.

Ares swung again.

She dodged the axes.

Energy blasted out again.

Denting his armour.

More energy blasts.

Throwing him against the wall.

She kept firing.

Ares hated this. He was pinned against the wall. He couldn't free himself.

The golden doors exploded open. The aliens must have reformed them when Ares wasn't looking.

Nineteen Angels stormed in. Firing at the woman.

She blasted energy out.

Slaughtering the Angels. Twisting their armour. Snapping bones.

Ares flew at the woman. No one fucking killed his Angels.

He grabbed her head.

Smashing it into the table.

Her head cracked.

Ares smashed her into the wall.

Her head bleed.

Ares grabbed her throat. Rose her high into the air. Snapping her spine over his knee and ripping her head off.

Ares just looked over at the pile of corpses of mutilated, twisted Angels that had come to save him. Ares wanted to recover their bodies but there was no time.

The male Nilihusian wanted to make the sun explode reducing the system to ash.

Ares had to stop him.

He had to get back to the Demigod and stop this once and for all.

CHAPTER 16

Georgia flat out couldn't believe how amazing it felt to have her perfect, stunning Lord of War back on board the Demigod. She had managed to slaughter the foul aliens in the orbital battle so that all that remained of their abominable blade-like warships were just flaming chunks of wreckage, but it was great to have Ares back onboard, so finally they could get some answers.

And stop this once and for all.

"Bring up a map of the system," Ares said as he rematerialised in the oval shaped bridge and went straight over to Georgia.

Ares even allowed a small smile to form on his lips as he studied Georgia's destruction through the immense floor-to-ceiling windows. Georgia just felt so powerful but she focused on the mission.

"Get to work," Georgia said to the command crew on their tiers of holographic computers.

Moments later a large red hologram of the entire

system appeared.

Georgia folded her arms. "All the worlds that were dark have returned to normal,"

That made no sense but after Ares quickly explained to everyone what he had found out on the capital world and the meeting over the freshly roasted governor, it actually did make sense.

"Commander," a command crew member said. "All planets show mass anti-Empire riots, murdering of any resistance left and burning down of Empire government buildings,"

Georgia waved him silent. That wasn't what was important at this moment in time and to be honest she wasn't that sure it ever would be. Riots and anti-Empire stuff wasn't really her department, that "honour" belonged firmly to the Arbiters.

Georgia would definitely be lying if she ever dared to say she wasn't just a bit concerned about all lives being lost each second that they wouldn't go and reinforce Empire forces.

"We need to know how the Triumvirate would destroy the sun," Ares said.

Georgia moved her hands about like she was some kind of witch in an effort to manipulate the hologram like Ares and Charlie had done, and she was just amazed that it worked.

The hologram zoomed in on the twenty closest planets to the sun in the system.

Ares gripped his battle-axes. "No. I doubt we're looking for a planet. Try something in orbit,"

Georgia just shook her head. There were trillions upon trillions of square miles to cover with a possible line of sight to the star. There were so many possibilities about where to hide a weapon.

Or was there?

"Scan the entire sector of the system," Georgia said. "Make sure all light levels are normal,"

Ares nodded in a strange superhuman way that if Georgia hadn't known Ares for as long as she had she might have mistaken it for disapproval. It was quite the opposite in a way.

"You think they're going to shroud whatever they're using," Ares said.

Georgia nodded. "It seems to fit their pattern. And as light travels through a vacuum consistently unless it is obscured by an object, say an orbital weapon platform, then we should be able to detect a difference,"

Ares looked really impressed, Georgia was so glad to be here. This was so much better than working for the Empire Army directly.

"Commander," a female command crew member said.

The hologram flashed a little and zoomed in on a tiny little speckle of darkness in orbit of the nearest planet to the sun.

It was amazing that metal wouldn't melt or something there, it was one of the few worlds in the systems that the Empire couldn't use because despite all their technology the world was simply too hot to do anything with.

Ares took a few steps forward. "Check the historical data for the trajectory of the planet,"

Georgia just focused on the actual position of the world and didn't get it.

"Confirmed my Lord," someone else said. "The world is thirty kilometres outside its normal orbit,"

Ares laughed just as Georgia realised what the hell was going on. The alien bastards weren't using a weapon per se to destroy to the sun. They were going to force an entire planet to smash into the sun and Georgia had absolutely no doubt the alien scum had put some kind of reactive weapons on the planet to help give the collision a little more apocalyptic power.

"Zoom in on the speckle," Georgia said.

The hologram zoomed in until it was too pixeled to see clearly but Georgia and Ares saw exactly what they needed to see. A massive perfectly flat platform in space with an immense laser cannon attached.

The laser cannon was typically used to stop asteroids destroying worlds but clearly that defensive idea was far too small.

Georgia guessed that the alien was planning to augment the cannon with its energy blasting powers but it was still dangerous.

They had to stop this alien now.

Georgia looked at Ares. "I'll grab my armour,"

Before Ares could protest she simply ran away to grab her battle armour. She wasn't staying out of this fight.

And the moment the fleet got a teleportation lock on the platform her and Ares were teleporting anyway.

And they were going to slaughter the alien. Stopping this once and for all.

CHAPTER 17

Ares rematerialised on the boiling hot metal platform with shadowy darkness surrounding him. He absolutely hated this alien with a passion and he so badly wanted to slaughter him.

"The fleet is staying docked and our teleporter homers are on," Georgia said.

That was very good news at least they would be able to teleport back at a moment's notice.

Ares hated the shadowy darkness that seemed to form a cage around the platform that was perfectly flat with only an immense cannon, easily a hundred metres tall, in the middle but it was glowing bright white light.

Ares recognised it instantly from the light that he had seen on the tower of corpses back on Nihilus 57.

Ares zoomed in on the cannon using his helmet's capability and noticed there were millions of tiny cones made from human bones attached to the cannon.

The cone had to be some kind of special symbol to the Nilihusians hence why they had arranged the corpses in the cone-like structure.

The entire platform hummed, popped and vibrated as Ares just knew that the cannon was charging up and the bright white light surrounding it grew in intensity.

An energy blast threw Ares forward.

He spun around mid-air. Whipping out his massive battle-axes.

Nothing was there. Georgia just looked at him like there was nothing going on.

Ares gestured they should go over to the cannon and Georgia nodded carefully scanning the platform with her automatic rifle.

Ares wasn't exactly sure how standard Empire Army war-gear would be effective here but Ares was hoping to be surprised.

The cannon got whiter and whiter, hotter and hotter.

It was about to fire.

Ares rushed over to it.

Ares swung his axes. Slicing into the metal of the cannon. It hummed louder.

Georgia screamed.

An energy blast threw Ares across the platform.

Ares tried to turn. He couldn't. Ares slammed into the floor.

Ares turned over. A perfectly naked humanoid man stood over him frowning.

Immense weight stopped Ares from moving his hands. His axes felt like lead. His superhuman strength failed him.

Georgia looked pinned to the ground to tens of metres from him.

The humanoid man, clearly the male member of the Triumvirate, grinned at Ares.

"You could have had everything," the man said. "I was burning an entire system for you. Think of all the trillions of souls you could have eaten,"

Ares hated this man. He was as crazy as they get and he just had to die.

"I am not your prophet," Ares said.

"Liar!" the man shouted. "You are the Lord of War. A god amongst the living. You could take the entire galaxy and universe for yourself,"

Ares had to admit he liked the sound of that. The Emperor was amazing but Ares could rule with an iron fist, he could be the greatest leader humanity had ever seen.

Ares shook his head. That wasn't the life designed for him.

"There is only one man who deserves that life. And his name is the Emperor!" Ares shouted.

Ares shot forward.

His axes became lighter.

Ares swung them.

The man's eyes widened. He shot out his lights.

Torrents of burning light shot out.

Pinning Ares against the cannon.

Beams of light shot out of the cannon. Wrapping around the world below it.

The platform screamed in protest. It surged forward. Dragging the world along with it.

The alien was going to kill them all.

Ares struggled. There was too much energy. Ares couldn't fight back.

The air got hotter. Superhuman sweat pooled at the bottom of Ares's armour.

The alien smiled.

Bullets screamed through the air.

The alien screamed. Shadowy blood splashed over Ares.

Ares surged forward.

The alien disappeared.

Ares screamed. Intense heat cooked the back of his head. His helmet turned white hot.

Ares spun around.

Swinging his axes.

The alien jumped on Ares's back.

His helmet started to melt.

The air got extremely hot.

Ares became lightheaded.

Bullets screamed through the air.

The alien hissed.

Ares swung his axes towards his head.

At the last possible second Ares changed course.

The axes just missed his head.

But as Ares felt them chomp onto solid he simply lifted up his axes and smiled at the shadowy humanoid corpses of the alien.

When the alien was truly dead its form flashed, flickered and changed into one of a massive beetle-like creature that just had to be burnt alive to stop it ever coming back.

Ares ripped off his largely melted helmet, just grateful his superhuman body was already pumping extreme levels of hormones, healing substances and drugs into his body to try and heal him faster.

Georgia aimed her automatic rifle at the top of the cannon and Ares went over with his axes.

Ares threw his axes as hard as he could. Georgia fired her bullets into the top of the cannon.

Ares's axes dented the top of the cannon and the bright white beams dragging the planet belong with them towards the sun stopped.

The planet seemed to shoot out away from them.

The platform jerked.

They were caught in the sun's gravitational pull.

The platform surged forward. Georgia collapsed from the heat.

Ares felt sweat pour into his armour.

He pressed a button on his armour. He didn't teleport away.

The connection failed.

Ares rushed over to Georgia. Cradling her in his arms.

He pressed her teleporter button. She teleported away.

Leaving Ares to die on the platform. Ares

couldn't die.

He had so much to do. He wanted to serve the Emperor. He wanted to rule the galaxy.

He-

Blinding white light forced Ares to shut his eyes. His skin bursted into flames.

Ares screamed in agony.

Then the light disappeared as Ares teleported away.

CHAPTER 18

Bright blinding stars shone like deadly diamonds through the icy cold void of space like treats a dangerous predator might lure children in with before taking them, because to Georgia that was exactly what humanity was in comparison to the grandeur and sheer majesty of space.

After returning from a rather tense few hours of blackjack where Georgia had won herself and an unholy amount of whiskey rations that she would almost certainly donate to the lesser members of her fleet, she just stood in the massive oval bridge just staring out at the darkness and deadly void of space.

No one else was inside the oval bridge, no one was hunched over their holographic computers on their tiers around the bridge, it was only her staring out the immense floor-to-ceiling windows.

Georgia couldn't completely believe what she had had to deal with on this particular mission. She had slaughtered enemies, killed rebels and fought in orbital battles before, but this time it just felt so different, and she now felt different as a person.

Despite the amazing aromas of sweet bitter coffee, grapefruit and rich chocolate that the command crew had been celebrating with before Georgia had ordered them to go on leave for the next few hours to celebrate their victory, Georgia just didn't feel like she was the same person.

She had come here in just delightful spirits that she was going to have the utter privilege of fighting with, serving and commanding the Lord of War's immense Angels of Death and Hope. And now that she had actually done that, she never ever wanted to go back to her normal Empire Army job again.

Sure in her Empire Army job she was one of the most influential commanders, she commanded an entire massive fleet of powerful warships, but over the past few days she had tasted and touched and loved real power.

And so what if the foul Nilihusian abominations had been wrong about Ares being the Lord of War from their prophecies, he could still do what they wished, commanded or expected of him.

If anyone was powerful enough to wage a war to end all wars against the glorious Emperor, it would be Ares. He was a true demigod amongst men and aliens and mutants alike, but what if Ares could become a god?

Georgia smiled at that idea, she had heard many stories from ancient Earth cultures about the children of gods and goddesses rising up against their parents. There was literally nothing stopping Ares from doing the same, it was actually even better than the legends of old, because the Emperor would never ever expect this so-called treachery.

For the Emperor was never a bad man, in fact he was the greatest, kindest and most superior human that had ever lived, but what if Ares could be greater?

Georgia slowly nodded to hear as the ship almost seemed to hum, pop and vibrate in agreement with her.

"Demigod," Georgia said grateful for Ares finally teaching her how to control the ship with just her voice and flicks of wrists. "Bring up the Nihilus system and plot a path to the Sol System,"

The ship hummed only and Georgia just smiled as the Nihilus system was only a few million lightyears away from Earth, and in all honesty, if Ares did want a secret rebellion against the Emperor, they would need a base.

"Bring the latest information about the riots and rebellion on the planets," Georgia said.

The red hologram changed to show footage of deadly raging infernos, Anti-Empire militia groups marching in the street killing all the loyalists they saw and the Arbiters engaging in fierce street fighting.

They were thankfully losing.

Georgia did just have to stop for a moment though and really think if this was what she wanted. In the Empire Army she was a master strategist, she had defeated "impossible" enemies with ease and won more battles than most Empire Army Lord Commanders oversaw in their lifetime.

If anyone could plot a course to victory, it would be her and she knew it.

"Demigod," Georgia said, "send a request to Earth, requesting I would like to lend my forces to the Arbiters' effort at stopping the Anti-Empire threat,"

As the ship hummed ever so slightly, Georgia knew that it was done and it wasn't hard to imagine Earth jumping at the chance for her impressive forces to help the Arbiters. But that would be earth's downfall, Georgia already had a good number of extremely loyal-to-her captains that she could send down to the rebellious worlds.

And she would be very firm in her orders for the forces to protect the rebels, but hide the facts that they were helping them, because that's the thing about rebellions, to do one Georgia and Ares would need an army.

So why not build on the Nilihusian's grand plan and use the rebellious humans to her own ends?

As the air grew cold, Georgia just smiled. The future was going to be very, very interesting and very bright if everything went to plan.

There was of course going to be a lot of work to do before she could reveal her rebellion, but she had little doubt Ares would at least listen to her idea, and if he refused, she would have to try and kill him, but she doubted it would ever come to that. Because she had been with Ares for too long and studied him for even longer to know that he was ambitious and there was only one real reason why he wanted to be and was the Emperor's favourite.

Because he wanted to be the Emperor's successor. He wanted to rule humanity for himself, so why in hell wouldn't she want to speed natural events along?

CHAPTER 19

Ares sat on a very large cold metal chair in the middle of a large box room with bright baby blue walls, a hovering grey desk in front of him and another two chairs on the other side of the desk. He had always liked its small appearance, the office, but considering he ever so rarely used it these days he had never seen the need to get art, sculptures or even a tub of rosemary, thyme and garlic.

The constant hum of the Demigod's engines, pop and crackling of the troops above him dancing and clubbing made Ares smile because it was truly amazing to know that his forces were celebrating and enjoying themselves. A happy crew was a good crew.

Ares still wasn't impressed with the lingering aroma of the command crew's bitter coffee that Ares just wanted to ban at his point, and it was even worse that the coffee left the strange taste of freshly baked coffee cake and walnuts on his tongue.

Thankfully the medical bay had been fully

operational after Ares had teleported away from the platform, and the amazing Angels with extensive medical training had managed to restore him to his former glory with perfectly repaired skin, face and the back of his head was fine too.

Ares was more than glad about that, but the real point of the mission was still running around in Ares's mind.

The entire point of the mission was to travel to the Nihilus system to investigate rebellions, the communication failures and the death of Angels, but it had quickly changed into something else.

The Nilihusians might have been monsters but they had proved that the Emperor had always bent the truth slightly. Ares was fairly sure he was forgetting and twisting the glorious Emperor's words but he was irritated that so many of his friends were dead so he needed to vent.

The Emperor had always claimed that humanity's best defence were the Angels of Death and Hope because they were the perfect killing machines and stronger, deadlier and tougher than any other human in the history of mankind.

But that was a lie.

Ares couldn't help but focus on how easily the Nilihusians had butchered the Angels from his own Legion and the legion of the Galaxy Burners. If Angels were really so tough and divine then surely that should have been impossible.

In fact the truth of the matter was that Ares had

to be the only true hope for humankind, because he had been the one to truly defeat the Nilihusians. They had laid waste to so many worlds, killed Angels and destroyed so much, but he had stopped them.

Not the Angels. Not the Emperor. Only he had with the help of a beautiful mortal woman.

Ares just bit his lip at that realisation, the Nilihusians had been right all along, he might not have been their prophet or whatever alien nonsense they dared to utter, but he could have it all.

After all, shouldn't the only hope for humanity be leading the species instead of being second in command?

"My Lord," Georgia said as she came into the office and sat down on one of the chairs facing Ares.

Ares was about to welcome her and congratulate her when he saw the evil, darkness and a sadist streak in her eyes.

Clearly Georgia was a much better human than Ares had ever predicted and studied and wanted. She was amazing and she had to be thinking along the same lines as him.

"I will make you my second in my command," Ares said, "if I became Emperor,"

Georgia smiled. "If? There is no *if* if we work together on this Lord Ares. We are the two brightest minds in the Empire, and we have fought the impossible that killed so many others. We can do this,"

Ares grinned at her points. She really did have a

beautiful twisted mind that would be so useful in the times to come, and she was right about everything.

"We need to go slow. Build up our forces carefully. Then we have to go quick before the Emperor can counter us," Ares said.

Georgia stood up and slowly nodded. "I have no doubt that is what we need to do but there will be time for that in the future. For today we rest and celebrate,"

Ares so badly wanted to protest or something, he wanted to start carving out a plan right now and he wanted to start burning away some of the corrupt deadweight on the Empire's body, but Georgia was sadly right.

No doubt the silly Emperor and the Emperor's Council would request visits, want to praise his actions and do so much rubbish that would inhibit his ability to plot and scheme their deaths. Yet Ares sadly knew that if he didn't wait for another mission before he set off again then that would draw suspicion.

And that was exactly the sort of thing he couldn't do now, because whilst he was definitely not scared of the darkness that was starting to claim his mind, body and soul, he just knew that if he wanted any chance to succeed, he needed to be careful, patient and contempt with the slow-moving nature of the Empire.

So whilst it was tomorrow's problems, and Ares fully intended to spend the rest of the day sharping his axes, studying languages and playing with his robot human project, it was still very much true that he was really looking forward to burning down the Empire to the ground and covering the galaxy in ashes so a Lord of War could rise from them once more and claim the galaxy for himself.

As that was his fate after all and Ares was never going to disrespect fate.

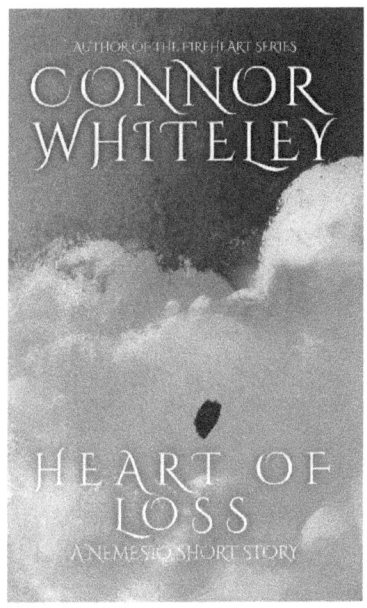

GET YOUR FREE AND EXCLUSIVE SHORT STORY NOW! LEARN ABOUT NEMESIO'S PAST!

https://www.subscribepage.com/fireheart

Keep up to date with exclusive deals on Connor Whiteley's Books, as well as the latest news about new releases and so much more!

Sign up for the Grab a Book and Chill Monthly newsletter, and you'll get one **FREE** ebook just for signing up: Agents of The Emperor Collection.

Sign Up Now!

https://dl.bookfunnel.com/f4p5xkprbk

About the author:

Connor Whiteley is the author of over 60 books in the sci-fi fantasy, nonfiction psychology and books for writer's genre and he is a Human Branding Speaker and Consultant.

He is a passionate warhammer 40,000 reader, psychology student and author.

Who narrates his own audiobooks and he hosts The Psychology World Podcast.

All whilst studying Psychology at the University of Kent, England.

Also, he was a former Explorer Scout where he gave a speech to the Maltese President in August 2018 and he attended Prince Charles' 70th Birthday Party at Buckingham Palace in May 2018.

Plus, he is a self-confessed coffee lover!

OTHER SHORT STORIES BY CONNOR WHITELEY

Mystery Short Stories:
A Smokey Way To Go
A Spicy Way To GO
A Marketing Way To Go
A Missing Way To Go
A Showering Way To Go
Poison In The Candy Cane
Christmas Innocence
You Better Watch Out
Christmas Theft
Trouble In Christmas
Smell of The Lake
Problem In A Car
Theft, Past and Team
Embezzler In The Room
A Strange Way To Go
A Horrible Way To Go
Ann Awful Way To Go
An Old Way To Go
A Fishy Way To Go
A Pointy Way To Go
A High Way To Go
A Fiery Way To Go
A Glassy Way To Go
A Chocolatey Way To Go

Kendra Detective Mystery Collection Volume 1
Kendra Detective Mystery Collection Volume 2
Stealing A Chance At Freedom
Glassblowing and Death
Theft of Independence
Cookie Thief
Marble Thief
Book Thief
Art Thief
Mated At The Morgue
The Big Five Whoopee Moments
Stealing An Election
Mystery Short Story Collection Volume 1
Mystery Short Story Collection Volume 2
Criminal Performance

Science Fiction Short Stories:
Gummy Bear Detective
The Candy Detective
What Candies Fear
The Blurred Image
Shattered Legions
The First Rememberer
Life of A Rememberer
System of Wonder

Lifesaver
Remarkable Way She Died
The Interrogation of Annabella Stormic
Blade of The Emperor
Arbiter's Truth
Computation of Battle
Old One's Wrath
Puppets and Masters
Ship of Plague
Interrogation
Edge of Failure
One Way Choice
Acceptable Losses
Balance of Power
Good Idea At The Time
Escape Plan
Escape In The Hesitation
Inspiration In Need
Singing Warriors
Knowledge is Power
Killer of Polluters
Climate of Death
The Family Mailing Affair
Defining Criminality
The Martian Affair
A Cheating Affair
The Little Café Affair

Mountain of Death
Prisoner's Fight
Claws of Death
Bitter Air
Honey Hunt
Blade On A Train
<u>Fantasy Short Stories:</u>
City of Snow
City of Light
City of Vengeance
Dragons, Goats and Kingdom
Smog The Pathetic Dragon
Don't Go In The Shed
The Tomato Saver
The Remarkable Way She Died
The Bloodied Rose
Asmodia's Wrath
Heart of A Killer
Emissary of Blood
Dragon Coins
Dragon Tea
Dragon Rider
Sacrifice of the Soul
Heart of The Flesheater
Heart of The Regent
Heart of The Standing
Feline of The Lost

Heart of The Story
City of Fire
Awaiting Death

Other books by Connor Whiteley:
Bettie English Private Eye Series
A Very Private Woman
The Russian Case
A Very Urgent Matter
A Case Most Personal
Trains, Scots and Private Eyes
The Federation Protects

Lord of War Origin Trilogy:
Not Scared Of The Dark
Madness
Burn It All

The Fireheart Fantasy Series
Heart of Fire
Heart of Lies
Heart of Prophecy
Heart of Bones
Heart of Fate

City of Assassins (Urban Fantasy)
City of Death
City of Marytrs
City of Pleasure
City of Power

Agents of The Emperor
Return of The Ancient Ones
Vigilance
Angels of Fire
Kingmaker
The Eight
The Lost Generation
Lord Of War Trilogy (Agents of The Emperor)
Not Scared Of The Dark
Madness
Burn It All Down

The Garro Series- Fantasy/Sci-fi
GARRO: GALAXY'S END
GARRO: RISE OF THE ORDER
GARRO: END TIMES
GARRO: SHORT STORIES
GARRO: COLLECTION
GARRO: HERESY
GARRO: FAITHLESS

GARRO: DESTROYER OF WORLDS
GARRO: COLLECTIONS BOOK 4-6
GARRO: MISTRESS OF BLOOD
GARRO: BEACON OF HOPE
GARRO: END OF DAYS

Winter Series- Fantasy Trilogy Books
WINTER'S COMING
WINTER'S HUNT
WINTER'S REVENGE
WINTER'S DISSENSION

Miscellaneous:
RETURN
FREEDOM
SALVATION
Reflection of Mount Flame
The Masked One
The Great Deer

Gay Romance Novellas
Breaking, Nursing, Repairing A Broken Heart
Jacob And Daniel
Fallen For A Lie
His Heartstopper

All books in 'An Introductory Series':
Careers In Psychology
Psychology of Suicide
Dementia Psychology
Forensic Psychology of Terrorism And Hostage-Taking
Forensic Psychology of False Allegations
Year In Psychology
BIOLOGICAL PSYCHOLOGY 3RD EDITION
COGNITIVE PSYCHOLOGY THIRD EDITION
SOCIAL PSYCHOLOGY- 3RD EDITION
ABNORMAL PSYCHOLOGY 3RD EDITION
PSYCHOLOGY OF RELATIONSHIPS- 3RD EDITION
DEVELOPMENTAL PSYCHOLOGY 3RD EDITION
HEALTH PSYCHOLOGY
RESEARCH IN PSYCHOLOGY
A GUIDE TO MENTAL HEALTH AND TREATMENT AROUND THE WORLD- A GLOBAL LOOK AT DEPRESSION
FORENSIC PSYCHOLOGY
THE FORENSIC PSYCHOLOGY OF THEFT, BURGLARY AND OTHER

CRIMES AGAINST PROPERTY
CRIMINAL PROFILING: A FORENSIC PSYCHOLOGY GUIDE TO FBI PROFILING AND GEOGRAPHICAL AND STATISTICAL PROFILING.
CLINICAL PSYCHOLOGY
FORMULATION IN PSYCHOTHERAPY
PERSONALITY PSYCHOLOGY AND INDIVIDUAL DIFFERENCES
CLINICAL PSYCHOLOGY REFLECTIONS VOLUME 1
CLINICAL PSYCHOLOGY REFLECTIONS VOLUME 2
Clinical Psychology Reflections Volume 3
CULT PSYCHOLOGY
Police Psychology

A Psychology Student's Guide To University
How Does University Work?
A Student's Guide To University And Learning
University Mental Health and Mindset

www.ingramcontent.com/pod-product-compliance
Lightning Source LLC
LaVergne TN
LVHW012113070526
838202LV00056B/5722